KING OTTER

JANE PORTER

SIMON & SCHUSTER

London   New York   Sydney   Toronto   New Delhi

Once, an otter found a box.

In it were fine clothes and fancy things.
He tried some on.

He felt taller . . . more exciting . . .
and extra-specially handsome.

He put on a crown, and looked in the mirror.

I am splendid, he thought.
I shall be KING Otter.

"Bow down before King Otter, hedgehogs," he said.

And they did.

Being King Otter was a fine thing.

A king needs somewhere important to sit, he thought.

"Squirrels! Build me a throne."

And it was built.

Otter sat back and surveyed his kingdom.
Everyone must see that I am king, thought Otter.

"There shall be a Grand Parade!"
he announced.

"With expert acrobats and musicians to delight your ears.

At the top of the hill, there will be a spectacular banquet, with seventeen types of cake in every colour.

You may all watch me eat.

And I shall travel in a golden coach pulled by unicorns.
Let the preparations commence!"

"But Otter," said a hedgehog, "unicorns don't really . . ."
"That will be all," said King Otter.

So the squirrels set to work with saws,

and the birds painted flags.

The frogs practised singing while doing handstands.

There was so much to do!

When the last buttercup garland was woven and the coach was ready, the Grand Parade began.

The golden coach sparkled as it bumped along, and King Otter waved to his people. Nobody had ever seen anything like it, and they couldn't help cheering.

Slowly, they climbed the hill. But the day was hot, and the coach and the king were heavy.

"Faster!" said King Otter. "Faster!"
The unicorns' horns started slipping off.

The king began to feel hungry. "We're going to be late for the banquet," he said. "Unicorns - start prancing." Nobody wanted to mention that they hadn't had time to make the cakes.

"Hurry up!" shouted the king.
The cheering stopped.

"I want my banquet

NOW!"

Suddenly, the silken ropes snapped.

The golden coach rolled down the hill until . . .

CRASH!

A wheel flew off, and King Otter
tumbled into the mud.

Otter sat up. "Birds! Come here!" he shouted.
"Squirrels! Rescue your king!"

But nobody came.

"This is treason!" he cried.
"Treachery!"

No one replied.

Otter put his muddy crown back on, but it felt all wrong.

He thought quietly
for a long time . . .

then took off all his fine things.
"You can be king now,"
he said to the tree stump.

He went to the river to wash his muddy paws,
and the water felt so good that he dived right in.

When Otter came up for air,
everything looked extra colourful.

He felt a tickle on his nose,

and sitting there was a butterfly,
twice as beautiful as the richest robe.

Around the bend, he found the others having fun.
"Excuse me," he said.

They all looked round.

"I think I may have been king too long," he said.
"Can I play with you now?"

"Of course," they said.

Otter's fine things weren't wasted.
The crown was handy for the squirrels' inventions.

The tassels on the jacket made the birds' nests rather glamorous.

And the box was the perfect stage for the frogs' shows.
Otter always cheers the loudest at the end.

And the boots?

Well, sometimes Otter puts them on again.

Just for fun.